MOUSSORGSKY

PICTURES AT AN EXHIBITION FOR THE PIANO

EDITED BY NANCY BRICARD

AN ALFRED MASTERWORK EDITION

Cover art: Project of Planning the Grand Gallery
of the Louvre
by Hubert Robert (1733–1808)
Louvre, Paris, France
© Réunion des Musées Nationaux / Art Resource, NY

MODEST MOUSSORGSKY

Contents

Foreword 3

    About This Edition 3

    Editorial Considerations 4

Background/Events 6

Musical Language 8

About *Pictures at an Exhibition* 9

    About Victor A. Hartmann 9

    About the Music. 9

Acknowledgments 15

PICTURES AT AN EXHIBITION

    Promenade 16

    Gnome 18

    Promenade 22

    The Old Castle 24

    Promenade 29

    Tuileries (Dispute of Children after Play) 29

    Cattle 33

    Promenade 36

    Ballet of the Unhatched Chicks 37

    "Samuel" Goldenberg and "Schmujle" 39

    Promenade 42

    Limoges. The Marketplace (The Big News) 44

    Catacombs (A Roman Burial Chamber) 49

    With the Dead in a Dead Language 50

    The Hut on Hen's Legs (Baba Yaga) 52

    The Bogatyr Gate (In the Ancient Capital, Kiev) 61

This edition is dedicated to the memory of Christopher Allan Burrows (1958–1999), whose love of life and music will always be an inspiration to me.

It is also dedicated to my beloved husband, Sherwyn M. Woods, M.D., Ph.D., whose continued love, support and encouragement made the production of this edition possible.

Nancy Bricard

Pictures at an Exhibition
Edited by Nancy Bricard

Foreword

ABOUT THIS EDITION

Pictures at an Exhibition is Modest Moussorgsky's (1839–1881) most important contribution to piano literature. It is unique in that few composers have had their works subjected to the editorial changes and arrangements that came about in an attempt to correct his "so-called" compositional weaknesses, and make his music conform to accepted conservatory formulas. The posthumous publication of this work made it impossible for Moussorgsky to protect the integrity of his composition. It is only in the latter half of the 20th century that serious efforts have been made to present the *Pictures at an Exhibition* in its original form. This critical edition addresses the sources and discrepancies between the various publications and the original autograph manuscript, as well as matters of tempo, pedaling, fingering, Moussorgsky's titles, and interpretation. Also included are essays on the historical, cultural and social environment that influenced Moussorgsky's art. This edition will supply relevant information to teachers, students and performing artists who wish to make informed musical decisions when faced with ambiguous or conflicting texts. In musical editions and scholarly publications, the composer's name appears in several different transliterations (e.g., Moussorgsky, Moussorgsky, Musorgsky, Mussorgski, Mussorgskij). The spelling "Moussorgsky" has been chosen for use in this edition and will supercede all other spelling variants.

The title page of the autograph manuscript appears with the following information neatly centered:

Dedicated to Vladimir Vasilyevich Stasov
"Pictures at an Exhibition"
In Memory of Victor Hartmann
M. Moussorgsky
1874

Stasov (1824–1906) was an art and music critic, propagandist, apologist, historian and the composer's close friend. In the lower left-hand corner is a note to Stasov: *"To you généralissime, the sponsor of the Hartmann Exhibition, in remembrance of our dear Victor, 27 June 74."* [1] This was probably when the manuscript was presented to Stasov. The name "Hartmann," which was possibly the original title, is written in pencil in the upper right-hand corner of the page (see the essay on Hartmann, page 9); although it was partially erased, it can still be read. Written in the lower right-hand corner is the following: *"for publication, Moussorgsky's signature, 26 July 74, Petrograd."* The autograph ends with Moussorgsky's signature and the exact date and place of completion: St. Petersburg, 22 June 1874 O.S. (O.S. stands for Old System Julian Calendar, which was 12 days behind the presently used Gregorian calendar. The Julian calendar was used in Russia until after the 1917 revolution when the Gregorian calendar, which had long been adopted by the rest of Europe, came into use.) The only existing manuscript of *Pictures at an Exhibition* is preserved in the Manuscripts Department of the Saltykov-Shchedrin State Public Library in Leningrad, Moussorgsky collection no. 502, archive no. 129. It consists of 26 pages, including the title page.

Pictures at an Exhibition was published in 1886, five years after the composer's death, by the firm of Vasily Bessel (1843–1907) of St. Petersburg. A second edition was later published by the same company, which included a preface by Stasov. Nicolay Rimsky-Korsakov (1844–1908) was the editor for both publications. He described his function:

I undertook to set in order and complete all of Moussorgsky's works and turn over gratis to the Bessel firm

Title page of the autograph manuscript of Pictures at an Exhibition.

[1] Modest Moussorgsky, *Pictures from an Exhibition*, facsimile publication of the autograph manuscript (Moscow: State Publishers Music, 1982), United States Library of Congress, Washington, DC.

those that I should find suitable for the purpose. For the next year-and-a-half or two years my work on my dead friend's compositions went on. [Moussorgsky's manuscripts] were in exceedingly imperfect order, there occurred absurd, incoherent harmonies, ugly part-writing, …illogical modulation, …ill-chosen instrumentation …in general; a certain audacious self-conceited dilettantism, at times moments of technical dexterity and skill but more often of utter technical impotence …publication without a skillful hand to put them in order would have had no sense save a biographical-historical one. If Moussorgsky's compositions are destined to live unfaded for 50 years after their author's death (when all his works will become the property of any and every publisher), such an archeologically accurate edition will always be possible, as the manuscripts went to the Public Library on leaving me.[2]

In making his changes, Rimsky-Korsakov totally ignored the composer's own statement:

With whatever shortcomings my music is born, with them it must live if it is to live at all.[3]

French critic and musicologist Jean Marnold (1859–1935) felt that Rimsky-Korsakov, *"by forcing his friend's music into a conservatory frock coat, had betrayed its essential genius."*[4]

The conductor Serge Koussevitzky (1874–1951) commissioned Maurice Ravel (1875–1937) to orchestrate the *Pictures at an Exhibition*, which was then published in 1922. Ravel used the Rimsky-Korsakov edition as a source, including Rimsky-Korsakov's alterations, such as substituting the dynamic marking of *p* for Moussorgsky's original *ff* at the beginning of *Cattle*. Ravel also added one measure in *The Old Castle*, and omitted the *Promenade* after *"Samuel" Goldenberg and "Schmuÿle."* *Pictures at an Exhibition* was finally published in its original version by the State Music Editions, Moscow, in 1939. The editor was Pavel Lamm, who edited the complete works of Moussorgsky.

There is no record of a public performance of *Pictures at an Exhibition* during Moussorgsky's lifetime. The first English performance was December, 1914 in London at the Musical Association Lecture on Moussorgsky by M. Montagu-Nathan (1877–1958), an English scholar of Russian Music. This performance coincided with the appearance of the English edition published by Augener Ltd.

EDITORIAL CONSIDERATIONS

Sources: This edition is based on the facsimile publication of the autograph manuscript, with a preface by Emilia Fried (Moscow: State Publishers Music, 1982), a copy of which resides in the Library of Congress. The Rimsky-Korsakov (Breitkopf & Härtel, 1983) as well as the Pavel Lamm (State Music Editions, Moscow, 1964) editions have been studied in depth. The following other editions, all based on either the autograph manuscript, the Rimsky-Korsakov, or the Pavel Lamm editions, have also been consulted:

—Augener Ltd., 1914, O. Thümer, editor
—C. F. Peters, 1921, Walther Niemann, editor
—Anton J. Benjamin, 1925, Otto Singer, editor
—Edward B. Marks Music Corporation, 1941, editor not identified
—G. Ricordi, 1949, Alfredo Casella, editor
—International Music Company, 1952, analytical foreword by Alfred Frankenstein
—C. F. Peters, 1982, Christoph Hellmundt, editor
—Wiener Urtext, Schott/Universal, 1984, Manfred Schandert and Vladimir Ashkenazy, editors
—G. Schirmer, 1992, editor not identified

Discrepancies: In this performance edition, the obvious errors such as missing sequential dots and articulation, and wrong pitches, are corrected in the score without adding parentheses. Decisions on controversial errors as well as other additions are placed in parentheses and, if necessary, the source or justification for these corrections or additions is explained with examples in site-specific footnotes along with alternative solutions. Notes, signs, slurs and symbols (such as warning accidentals) have been added by the editor in parentheses. Looking at the autograph, it is very difficult at times to ascertain where Moussorgsky's slurs begin or end, and his use of staccato marks and other interpretive markings are often inconsistent. The autograph will take precedence when controversy or doubt exists as to possible or presumed errors in Moussorgsky's original

[2] Nikolay Rimsky-Korsakov, *My Musical Life*, trans. Judah A. Joffe (New York: Vienna House, 1974 [© 1942]), revised edition (London: Ernst Eulenberg Ltd., 1974), 248–249.

[3] Milton Cross, *Encyclopedia of the Great Composers and Their Music*, vol. II (New York: Doubleday & Company, Inc., 1953), 552.

[4] Caryl Emerson and Robert William Oldani, *Modest Musorgsky and Boris Godunov* (Cambridge, MA: Cambridge University Press, 1994), 159.

notation. Rimsky-Korsakov's principal alterations appear in the footnotes and at times in the score when the editor feels that they reflect Moussorgsky's intentions. This format has been used not only for the purpose of clarity, but also because of the pedagogical principle that a student's correct first reading of the score is exceedingly important as it makes a lasting auditory and haptic impression that is difficult to change.

Tempo: Metronome markings were taken from a letter dated January 31, 1903 from Stasov to Arkady Mikhailovich Kerzin (1857–1914), founder and director of the Kerzin Moscow Circle of Lovers of Russian Music in England. In this letter, Stasov explained that he met with Rimsky-Korsakov at a supper in honor of the German conductor Max Fiedler (1859–1939) at the home of composer Alexander Glazunov (1865–1936). There, Stasov and Rimsky-Korsakov discussed the tempos of the pieces of *Pictures at an Exhibition*:

> *We sat down at the piano, Rimsky-Korsakov played each number over a few times, and then we recalled how our Moussorgsky had played them—remembered, tried them, and, finally, fixed the right tempi with the aid of a metronome.*[5]

O. Thümer, editor of the Augener Ltd. 1914 edition, was the first to publish the metronome markings. They can also be found in the International Music Company edition. There were, however, three obvious errors, which probably occurred in translation or engraving. The tempo markings for *Cattle* should have been ♪ = 88, not ♩ = 88; *Ballet of the Unhatched Chicks* ♩ = 88, not ♩. = 88; *The Bogatyr Gate* ♩ = 84, not ♩. = 84. These errors in note values have been corrected in this score. In some instances this editor has questioned the recollections of Stasov and Rimsky-Korsakov, and has suggested tempos, which appear within parentheses.

Pedaling: Moussorgsky's pedal markings are few and are found only in *"Samuel" Goldenberg and "Schmuÿle," The Hut on Hen's Legs* and the *The Bogatyr Gate*. These are notated in the score as 🎵. and are placed exactly in the location that they appear in the autograph. There are no pedal release markings. All other pedal marks (└────^────┘) are editorial.

Fingering: Moussorgsky did not supply any fingerings in *Pictures at an Exhibition*; however, in *The Hut on Hen's Legs*, measures 108–109 and 112–113, top staff, he did indicate *m.s.* (*mano sinistra:* left hand). Many editorial *divisi* and fingerings have been added, not only to aid in the technical and interpretive aspects of the music, but also to facilitate difficult passages for pianists with small hands. Alternate fingerings are also given and are separated by a horizontal line or illustrated in the footnotes. It is often helpful to first practice a passage with the given fingerings until it can be played up to tempo. Some fingerings work very well at a slow tempo, but not at the actual tempo of the piece. If a fingering does not seem to work at tempo, one should try the alternate fingering and *divisi*. As a matter of personal preference, I almost always change fingers when repeating expressive notes. These notes should vary in nuance and I feel that changing the fingers helps to produce these shades of difference. This opinion, however, is not shared by all pianists. Many prefer using the same finger on repeated expressive notes for the purpose of developing finger sensitivity and maintaining maximum control. Changing from one finger to another (finger substitution) on a note is marked, for example, as 3-5. Numbers are circled to indicate using more than one finger on a note ㉜. I often use multiple fingers on a single note as it not only facilitates the production of a different kind of sound but also aids in isolating a note to give it the intended character.

Titles: Moussorgsky's titles in this score are translated into English. His original multi-lingual titles appear in the following languages and are given in the footnotes: French, German, Yiddish, Latin, Italian, Polish, and Russian.

---

[5] M. Montagu-Nathan, "New Light on Moussorgsky's Pictures," *Monthly Musical Record* 47 (May 1917): 105–6.

Background/Events

Moussorgsky's lifetime was marked by significant personal, historic, political and cultural events that had a decided impact on his well being and art. One such event was the rise of nationalism, which began in 1836 with the performance of Mikhail Glinka's (1804–1857) patriotic opera *Life for the Czar* and quickly spread to artistic areas other than opera. Another occurrence was the emancipation of the serfs in 1861. A visit to Moscow in 1859 set the stage for his deep involvement with Russian history and the spirit and life of its people. In a letter to fellow composer Mili Balakirev (1837–1910), he wrote:

> *You know I have been a cosmopolitan, but now I have undergone a sort of rebirth: I have been brought near to everything Russian.*[6]

The Marquis de Custine (1790–1857), a French aristocrat, journeyed through Imperial Russia in 1839, the year of Moussorgsky's birth. He wrote a travel account of this trip, which became a bestseller. On the subject of Russian art he wrote the following commentary:

> *The Russians have not yet reached the point of civilization at which there is real enjoyment of the arts. At present their enthusiasm on these subjects is pure vanity; it is a pretense, like their passion for classic architecture. Let these people look within themselves, let them listen to their primitive genius, and, if they have received from Heaven a perception of the beauties of art, they will give up copying, in order to produce what God and nature expect from them.*[7]

His wish came about with the rise of nationalism. Russians were tired of importing and imitating ideas in art, literature and music from Europe, and now needed a renaissance with a distinctive Slavic character. Russia possessed a wealth of folk songs, liturgical music and fairy tales that could serve as an inspiration for composers and give their music a national character. Established composers Glinka and Alexander Dargomizhsky (1813–1869) prepared the groundwork for a Russian national music school by exploiting these assets. A fervent advocate of this musical nationalism, Moussorgsky became a member of a group whose main goal was to spearhead this trend. The group was called the *moguchaya kuchka* (mighty little heap) by Stasov, who was the group's ideological leader. They were also identified as the *Mighty Five* or the *Russian Five*. Members of the group were Balakirev, César Cui (1835–1918), Alexander Borodin (1833–1887), Moussorgsky and Rimsky-Korsakov. Balakirev was the only professional musician among them. The rest were amateurs with no formal technical training. Moussorgsky was perhaps the most original of the group and it is interesting to note that he is the only one who never left Russia. Stasov characterized the *Mighty Five* as follows:

> *Balakirev was the most inspired; Cui, the most graceful; Rimsky-Korsakov, the most learned; Borodin, the most profound; and Moussorgsky, the most talented.*[8]

Besides the *Mighty Five*, this era also produced many other great artists. Among these were Nikolay Gogol (1809–1852), who laid the foundation for literary realism, the sculptor Mark Antokolsky (1842–1902), the painter Il'ia Repin (1844–1930), and the architect Victor Hartmann (1834–1873).

This spirit of nationalism inspired the need for a school of music. Until 1860, there were no music schools as musicians were not recognized as a having legitimate professions. Accordingly, two conservatories with opposing ideologies were established in St. Petersburg in 1862. The first was the St. Petersburg Conservatory, which was founded by Anton Rubinstein (1829–1894). It used the European conservatories as its model, employing only German instructors. The other was the Free Music School, which was founded by Balakirev. This school reflected the aspirations of Stasov and the *Mighty Five*. In 1866, Anton Rubinstein's brother Nikolai (1835–1881) founded the Moscow Conservatory. These events were extremely important to musicians, giving them status as teachers, performers and composers.

Russia's great national pride and patriotism that grew after the defeat of Napoleon in 1812 was dealt a severe blow with her defeat in the Crimean War (1853–56) against Great Britain, France and Turkey. This defeat was due in part to an inept military command and the inability to mobilize and transport troops and supplies. Russia was not ruled by law but by the autocracy of the czars in the form of edicts (*ukase*), and their use of the army and the police. The need for modernization and reforms was evident. For this to be accomplished, serfdom had to end. This legalized bondage was comparable to American slavery in that the serfs were owned and could be bought and sold. In March 1856, Czar Alexander II (1818–1881) made the following statement to the nobility in Moscow concerning the problem:

> *It is better to abolish serfdom from above than to wait until the serfs begin to liberate themselves from below.*[9]

[6] *New Grove's Dictionary of Music and Musicians*, 1980 ed., s.v. "Musorgsky, Modest Petrovich."

[7] Marquis de Custine, *Empire of the Czar: A Journey through Eternal Russia*, a recent reprint edition of the first anonymously translated English version of 1843 (New York: Anchor-Doubleday, 1989), 206.

[8] *Moussorgsky Remembered*, comp. and ed. Alexandra Orlova, trans. Véronique Zaytzeff and Frederick Morrison (Bloomington, IN: Indiana University Press, 1991), 133.

[9] *The New Encyclopaedia Britannica, Macropaedia, Knowledge in Depth*, 15th ed. (1995), s.v. "Russia and the Soviet Union, History of" (under the subsection "From Alexander II to Nicholas II").

The Emancipation Proclamation was issued by Alexander II on February 19, 1861:

Declare to all our loyal subjects…

…All those people now bound to the soil will receive at the proper time the full rights of free rural residents.

…The landowners, maintaining their possession of all lands now belonging to them will place at the disposal of the peasants a certain quantity of field soil and other lands according to given regulations…[10]

This manifesto became law in 1863 and had a tremendous impact on the lives and fortunes of the landowners. Moussorgsky lost the monetary security he had as the son of a wealthy landowner. He and his brother Filaret were financially ruined because of this loss of income from the family estates and Modest was forced to go to work for the civil service. Nevertheless, this did not affect his interest, sympathy and love for the peasant. He harbored no ill will or malice toward them. He, in fact, had peasant blood as his paternal grandmother was a serf. In a letter to Balakirev, dated June 10, 1863, he voiced his reaction to the reform:

There's nothing to write about myself, and one shouldn't chatter nonsense; I have no impressions to give you, for what impressions could there be in Pskov Prov., which in my own district I know by heart with all its blessed landowners. I can say one thing only: the peasants are far more capable than the landlords in the matter of self-government—in their meetings they bring their business straight to the point, and in their own way they ably discuss their own interests; while the landlords in assemblies quarrel among themselves, acquire swelled heads—while the aim of the meeting and the business in hand are shoved to the side.[11]

Around this time the term *intelligentsia* came into use. This term described a group of people with a good education and political and social consciousness. They were, in general, opposed to existing systems and advocated change. Moussorgsky, following the example of many of the young Russian *intelligentsia*, joined a commune in 1863. He lived in an apartment with five other young men who enthusiastically exchanged ideas on art, literature, history, science, theology, philosophy and politics. They were influenced in their thinking by Nikolai Chernyshevsky (1829–1889), a socialist writer, nihilist and a champion of artistic realism, who stated: *"True beauty resides in life and the primary purpose of art is to reproduce reality."*[12] Leo Tolstoy (1828–1910) was also influenced by the writings of Chernyshevsky, and, although he and Moussorgsky did not know each other, they shared similar views. Tolstoy predicted:

The artist of the future will be free of all perversions of technical camouflage concealing the absence of subject matter, and who, not being a professional artist, and receiving no payment for his activity, will produce art only when he feels compelled to do so by an irresistible inner impulse.[13]

All these events had a profound effect in shaping Moussorgsky's art. Unfortunately, his life was extremely unstable and his mental and physical health deteriorated dramatically after the death of his mother in 1865. Much has been made of his alcoholism, but many of his symptoms were due to a continuing battle with epilepsy. The last month of his life was spent in the Nikolayevsky Military Hospital. It was there that Repin painted the famous portrait of Moussorgsky during a temporary improvement in Moussorgsky's health. On March 16, 1881, Moussorgsky died in abject poverty there and was buried in the Alexander Nevsky cemetery in St. Petersburg.

Portrait of Moussorgsky shortly before his death in 1881 by Il'ia Repin (1844–1930)

[10] *The Musorgsky Reader*, ed. and trans. Jay Leyda and Sergei Bertensson (New York: W. W. Norton & Company, Inc., 1947), 36.
[11] Ibid., 37.

[12] Michael Russ, *Musorgsky: Pictures at an Exhibition* (Cambridge, MA: Cambridge University Press, 1992), 9.
[13] Victor Seroff, *Modest Moussorgsky* (New York: Funk & Wagnalls, 1968), 119.

Musical Language

Shortly before his death, Moussorgsky wrote an auto-biographical sketch for Hugo Riemann's (1849–1919) music dictionary stating his position as a composer:

> *Moussorgsky cannot be classed with any existing group of musicians, either by the character of his compositions or by his musical views. The formula of his artistic "profession de foi" may be explained by his view of the function of art: art is a means of communicating with people, not an aim in itself. This guiding principle has defined the whole of his creative activity. Proceeding from the conviction that human speech is strictly controlled by musical laws (Virchow, Gervinus), he considers the function of art to be the reproduction in musical sounds not merely of feelings, but first and foremost of human speech. Acknowledging that in the realm of art only artist-reformers such as Palestrina, Bach, Gluck, Beethoven, Berlioz and Liszt have created the laws of art, he considers these laws as not immutable but liable to change and progress, like everything else in man's inner world.*[14]

These ideas evolved directly from Dargomizhsky who wanted "truth" in music. Truth to Moussorgsky was the wish to identify his compositions with the lives of the Russian people and nourish his art on events that affected them. He wished to portray human experience by "speaking" honestly and convincingly through his music in a language as denuded and rudimentary as possible. This concept was *realism*. Moussorgsky's *realism* was in the way he treated his subjects, not his choice of subjects. Caryl Emerson and Robert Oldani said that, *"Certainly, Moussorgsky is a realist, but his power lies not in the fact that his music is realistic but in the fact that his realism is music in the most staggering sense of the word."*[15] Being a "self-taught" composer, he could rely on his intuition and instincts unhampered by a theoretical education. Perhaps he was afraid that the technique of following the rules of composition would ruin his originality, so he preferred to remain ignorant. Claude Debussy (1862–1918) had this to say about Moussorgsky's music: *"It looks like the art of an inquisitive savage who would discover music at each step set by his emotion."*[16]

There are no set formulas in his music and no definite forms. Michel D. Calvocoressi (1877–1944), writer and critic, said: *"for creating forms, one must be master of forms."*[17] Moussorgsky's *realism* started with the raw elements but he did not have the means to organize them. His harmony is quite free, new and beautiful with bold modulations and unusual chord progressions. His melodies have a modal character appropriated from orthodox religious music which effects the harmony. His vocal writing was both lyrical and at the same time represents the accents and patterns of human speech. There is a mixture of both the primitive and the refined in his music. Some of the ugly sounds and awkward writing are due to ignorance but some are definitely designed for special effects. Nevertheless, his compositions are original and spontaneous works of art marked with simple eloquence, sensitivity, insight and a strong personality.

In a letter dated December 24, 1877 from Tchaikovsky (1840–1893) to Nadezhda von Meck, Tchaikovsky said:

> *Moussorgsky you are quite correct in characterizing as hopeless. His talent is perhaps the most remarkable of all these (the Balakirev group). But he has a narrow nature, is totally devoid of desire for self-improvement, and is deluded by a blind faith in the absurd theories of his circle and in his own genius. In addition, he has some sort of low nature, which loves all that is coarse, crude, and rough. He is, in short, the direct antithesis of his friend Cui, who, though he swims in the shallows, is at any rate always decorous and graceful, whereas Moussorgsky coquets with his illiteracy and takes pride in his ignorance, rolling along, blindly believing in the infallibility of his genius. But he has a real, and even original, talent which flashes out now and then… A Moussorgsky, for all his ugliness, speaks a new language. Beautiful it may not be, but it is fresh.*[18]

After Moussorgsky's death, Claude Debussy summed up Moussorgsky's great talent and compositions:

> *…It is apparent from these dates [Moussorgsky was born in 1839 and died in 1881] that to become a genius he had little time to lose. And indeed he lost none, and he will leave an indelible impression on the minds of those who love him or will come to love him. No one has ever appealed to the best in us in a deeper and more tender expression. He is unique and will remain so, for his art is free from artifice and arid formulas. Never was refined sensitivity interpreted by such simple means. It is like the art of a wild creature who discovers music in each of his emotions. Neither is there ever a question of a definite form; or rather, this form is so manifold that it cannot possibly be likened to the recognized or orthodox forms. It is achieved by little consecutive touches linked by a mysterious bond and by his gift of luminous intuition. Sometimes, too, Moussorgsky produces the effect of shuddering, restless shadows, which close around us and fill the heart with anguish.*[19]

---

[14] *New Grove's Dictionary*, s.v. "Musorgsky, Modest Petrovich."

[15] Emerson and Oldani, 156.

[16] Louis Aguettant, *La Musique de Piano, Des Origines à Ravel* (Paris: Éditions Albin Michel, 1954), 342.

[17] Ibid., 344.

[18] Leyda and Bertensson, 366–367.

[19] Seroff, 136–137.

About *Pictures at an Exhibition*

ABOUT VICTOR A. HARTMANN

Victor Alexandrovich Hartmann, the son of a military doctor, was born in St. Petersburg on April 23 O.S., 1834. Both parents died before he was four and his care was taken over by an aunt who was married to a St. Petersburg architect. Through her influence, he was admitted to the Imperial Academy of Mines and after six years placed in the Academy of Fine Arts, where his progress was quite outstanding. After two years of practical work, he went on a foreign tour at the government's expense. During that period, Hartmann produced the majority of watercolors and scenes of life sketches that inspired Moussorgsky. Six of these sketches were part of the ten *Pictures at an Exhibition*. Hartmann's name is known mainly from this association. The American author, music and art critic Alfred Frankenstein (1906–1981) pointed out that although Hartmann's pictures are skillful, they are far from extraordinary. They provide insight into the imaginative and creative processes whereby the visual conceptions of a man of talent may be turned into the tonal conceptions of a man of genius.[20]

Although his profession was that of an architect, his main interest was in painting and sketching. Victor Hartmann was also known as an ornamentalist, designer and watercolorist. Architecture, as we know it, is the art of adapting and designing a structure for a certain use and to occupy a specific space. For Hartmann it seems to have meant changing one form of surface ornamentation to another more elaborate and, for the most part, impractical, totally useless and somewhat artificial. He was striving for an original national architectural style based on Russian folk materials. Ivan Kramskoi (1837–1887), a leading realist artist wrote:

> It always seemed to me that Hartmann was not an architect in the precise sense of the word but just an artist, and a fantastic one at that …Hartmann was no ordinary man. He could have been completely ignored if the time had not put forward a demand for grand architectural projects such as world fairs. When he was to build commonplace, utility objects, Hartmann was a failure, for he needed fairytale castles and fantastic palaces for which there were no precedents—here he could create truly wonderful things.[21]

His work was ephemeral in the sense that so much of it was directed towards constructing buildings for fairs, monuments and decorative projects. The Russian Millenary Monument, commemorating the 1,000 year founding of the Russian State, was erected in 1862 at Novgorod, now known as Gorki. It is the only example left of his architectural endeavors. Of the 400 works that Moussorgsky viewed at his Memorial Exhibition, less than 100 can be accounted for today. Hartmann also made designs for handicrafts and for the theater.

Three years before Hartmann's death, Stasov became his patron and a champion of his work.

> In my eyes he [Hartmann] was the most talented, the most original, the most adventurous, the boldest of all our architects, even those of the new young school …Of course I considered him rather inferior to Moussorgsky, Repin and Antokolsky, however, he was a talent—strong!![22]

Stasov introduced Hartmann to writers, painters, sculptors, poets and musicians who would gather in his home. It was probably there that Hartmann met Moussorgsky in 1870, and thus began their close friendship. They were both ardent nationalists and were seeking new directions; however, they also differed in many ways. Hartmann seemed to lack the strong social commitment and concerns of Moussorgsky, and the ornamental nature of his work contrasted sharply with the stark realism found in Moussorgsky's music. Hartmann died very suddenly at the age of 39, apparently of an aneurysm. It was a terrible loss for Moussorgsky, especially since he felt in part responsible because he did not recognize the symptoms of a previous attack, which had occurred while walking home with him. A Hartmann Memorial Exhibition of his paintings, drawings, sketches and designs was organized by Stasov with the help of Count Paul Suzor, president of the St. Petersburg Architectural Association. It was held in the late winter and spring of 1874 in the rooms of the Architectural Association building. Moussorgsky visited this exhibition and then composed his cycle. *Pictures at an Exhibition* represents his resolve to pay homage to his beloved friend by recreating his paintings and drawings in a set of musical illustrations.

ABOUT THE MUSIC

Pictures at an Exhibition was written in a very short period of time. In a letter written in June of 1874 to Vladimir Stasov, Moussorgsky wrote of his progress:

> My dear généralissime,
>
> Hartmann[23] is boiling as Boris [his opera Boris Godunov] boiled—the sounds and the idea hung in the air, and now I am gulping and overeating, I can hardly manage to scribble it down on paper. Am writing four numbers—with good transitions [on Promenade]. I want to do it as quickly and steadily as possible. My physiognomy can be seen in the intermezzi. I consider it successful so far. I embrace you and I take it that you bless me—so give me your blessing!
>
> Musoryanin[24]
>
> V[otre] S[erviteur][25]

In Moussorgsky's *Pictures at an Exhibition*, the culture and emotions of the Russian people are seen through a musical lens trained on Hartmann's suggestive scenes. Even though some of

---

[20] Alfred Frankenstein, "Victor Hartmann and Modeste Musorgsky," *The Musical Quarterly* XXV/3 (July 1939): 269.

[21] Emilia Fried, preface to the printed facsimile publication of the autograph manuscript (Moscow: State Publishers Music, 1982), Library of Congress, Washington, DC.

[22] Michael Russ, 15.

[23] *Hartmann* was the title originally intended for the cycle.

[24] Moussorgsky signed several letters to his intimate friends in this way. It is an old Slavic way to pronounce his name.

[25] Leyda and Bertensson, 271.

these sketches reflect countries and people Hartmann viewed in his travels abroad, Moussorgsky has infused into them a unifying Russian component. His music speaks to us of fairy tales, the drama of everyday life, death, animals, human personalities, children, and monuments in a dialogue that is simple, direct and unrestricted by traditional rules and conventions. One has the impression of "hearing" reality. Russian émigré musicologist and author Alexandra Orlova wrote:

> The piano suite Kartinki s vystavki [Pictures from an Exhibition] is one of Moussorgsky's greatest works. It is far from being a simple "illustration" of Hartmann's drawings. It is a profoundly philosophical work, a meditation on life and death, on history, on the people, and on man in general.[26]

Moussorgsky did not use the sonata form and there is no development of themes. Although there is no pure counterpoint in the *Pictures at an Exhibition*, there is linear movement in some of the *Promenades* and in "Samuel" Goldenberg and "Schmuÿle" that suggests counterpoint. Binary and ternary forms are generally preferred by Moussorgsky. The clearest example of his use of ternary forms are found in the *Ballet of the Unhatched Chicks* (where he uses the instrumental form of Scherzino and Trio) and *The Hut on Hen's Legs*. Chords are not striking in themselves but chord progressions are often innovative. The rhythms are varied, driven and sometimes obsessive. At times the writing for the piano is awkward. He uses all the capabilities and resources of the piano to produce a variety of sounds but is obviously more interested in the resulting sonorities than the technique of creating them. However, there are some pianistic moments such as in *Tuileries, Limoges,* and *The Hut on Hen's Legs*. There is very little of the usual ornamentation such as arpeggios. Trills are used sparingly: in *Gnomes*, to produce a low, rumbling effect, and in *Ballet of the Unhatched Chicks*, to give the effect of fluttering feathers.

An interpreter of this work must project its diverse elements with clarity, vividness and an emotional empathy for Russia and its people. One must also possess a sensitivity to color, nuance and poetic imagery to portray the various characters and episodes in a realistic and convincing manner. It is very important to "see" Hartmann's various pictures through the eyes of Moussorgsky and understand the stories they tell through his music.

In the first edition, published by Bessel, Vladimir Stasov wrote brief comments on the contents of the cycle. These comments are given in italics, along with additional remarks by this editor in the following descriptions of the pieces in *Pictures at an Exhibition*.

---

[26] Orlova, 173–174.

Promenades/Intermezzi . . . . (listed below)

Stasov's comment: *The introduction has the name* Promenade.

In the autograph manuscript, the title *Promenade* is given to the introductory theme (page 16). This theme recurs six times thereafter throughout the composition in variations of different colors and character. The first three recurrences (pages 22, 29 and 36) are without titles; Moussorgsky referred to them in his letter of June 1874 to Stasov as *Intermezzi*.[27] The fourth recurrence is titled *Promenade* (page 42) and has the same characteristics as the introductory *Promenade*. The fifth is incorporated into *With the Dead in a Dead Language* (page 50) and the sixth recurrence is incorporated into *The Bogatyr Gate* (page 65, measures 97–104).

Promenade, *measures 1–19, in which the key signature accidentals and pitches are written consistent with the alto clef*

On the first page of the introductory *Promenade* in the autograph (measures 1–19), it is interesting to note that Moussorgsky had written treble and bass clefs, but both the placement of the accidentals in the key signatures and the pitches are appropriate to the alto or C clef. Beginning on the second page (measures 20 to the end), Moussorgsky's key signatures and pitches are written compatible with the treble and bass clefs. It was most likely Rimsky-Korsakov who first discovered this mistake in the autograph and corrected it prior to the first publication. Although many musicians, scholars and editors have studied the autograph in depth, to my knowledge, no one has acknowledged this error. One can only speculate over Moussorgsky's actual intentions.

---

[27] *Musorgsky Reader*, 271.

The music of the first and the ensuing *Promenades* depicts Moussorgsky as he walks back and forth from one painting to another. The rhythmic alternation between 5/4 and 6/4 illustrates the awkward and clumsy gait of the portly composer who weighed well over 200 pounds. The recurring *Promenades* give structure to the cycle and serve as interludes that bind the *Pictures at an Exhibition* together. The theme is totally independent of Hartmann's material and appears in variations that convey Moussorgsky's moods and feelings as he moves from picture to picture. Although the second, third and fourth recurrence of the theme have been titled *Promenades* in this and most other editions, they are untitled in the autograph. These same *Promenades/Intermezzi* are written without key signatures, the accidentals having been incorporated into the music. In the autograph, the fifth *Promenade* restates the introduction, is titled *Promenade*, and is given a key signature. This *Promenade* is omitted by Ravel in his orchestration, an omission that detracts from the balance of the work in the opinion of this editor. The *attacca* (continue immediately to the next section or movement without a break) markings at the end of each *Promenade* were omitted by Rimsky-Korsakov as well as many subsequent editions.

Gnome 18

Original title in Latin: *Gnomus*
Stasov's comment: *Sketch representing a little gnome clumsily walking on deformed legs.*

Hartmann's design was a carved wooden nutcracker for a Christmas tree. The ornament was in the shape of a gnome and a nut was put into his mouth to crack.

Emilia Fried says:

> *Moussorgsky's piece is grotesque, with a touch of tragedy, a convincing example of the "humanization" of a ridiculous prototype. In the music, which portrays the dwarf's awkward leaps and bizarre grimaces, are heard cries of suffering, moans and entreaties. The gnome is related to other characters in Moussorgsky's works where behind an ugly outward appearance one senses a living and suffering soul [in particular, the song* Darling Savvishna].[28]

This character anticipates the future *Scarbo* in Ravel's *Gaspard de la Nuit.*

The Old Castle 24

Original title in Italian: *Il vecchio Castello*
Stasov's comment: *A medieval castle before which stands a singing troubadour.*

The Italian title suggests that this was one of Hartmann's watercolor sketches done in Italy. He was traveling through Western Europe studying architecture at the time. Built over a G-sharp pedal point that continues throughout the entire piece and sustains its continuity, the melody is modal, very flowing and beautiful.

Tuileries (Dispute of Children after Play) 29

Original title in French: *Tuileries (Dispute d'enfants après jeux)*
Stasov's comment: *A walk in the Tuileries gardens with a group of children and nursemaids.*

Moussorgsky mistakenly spelled *Tuileries* as *Tuilleries* in the autograph. The "voices" of the noisy children as they play and quarrel together and the admonishments of their nana are clearly heard in this musical picture. *Tuileries* is an example of Moussorgsky's ability to portray the world of children; he understood them and loved their creative imaginations and sincerity. This interest is seen in other compositions, notably *The Nursery*, a group of songs for voice and piano. *In the Corner*, the second piece of that cycle, was dedicated to Hartmann.

Cattle 33

Original title in Polish: *Bydlo*
Stasov's comment: *A Polish wagon on enormous wheels is drawn by oxen.*

The locale for this picture is Sandomir, an ancient city in Poland with many architectural monuments, which Hartmann visited before his return to Russia. There he painted many scenes of life in the Jewish ghetto. The melody is a folk song, presumably sung by the driver. Emilia Fried felt that it contained more Ukrainian rather than Polish national elements. Heavy, reiterated left-hand chords that depict a huge cart rumbling down the road accompany it. Moussorgsky intended the appearance of the wagon to be a surprise, which is why the cart is not named in the title and there is a *ff* at the beginning. He wrote to Stasov: *"Right between the eyes 'Sandomirzsko bydlo' (le télégue) it stands to reason that le télégue isn't named, but this is between us."*[29] *Le télégue* is a Moussorgsky "Frenchification" of *telega*, a Russian cart. Rimsky-Korsakov ruined this surprise by changing Moussorgsky's original dynamic to a *p*.

---

[28] Fried, preface to facsimile of the autograph manuscript.

[29] Leyda and Bertensson, 272.

Sketches of Costumes for J. Gerber's Ballet Trilby
Watercolor by Victor A. Hartmann

Ballet of the Unhatched Chicks 37

Original title in Russian: *Balet Nevylupivshikhsya Ptentsov*
Stasov's comment: *Hartmann's sketch of ballet costumes for a picturesque scene of the ballet* Trilbi.

This watercolor sketch is one of the few remaining examples of Hartmann's work as a stage and costume designer and is preserved in Leningrad. The Exhibition Catalog describes it as *"Canary-chicks, enclosed in eggs as in suits of armor. Instead of a head dress, canary heads put on like helmets, down to the neck."*[30] The score is written in the upper registers of the piano and skillfully imitates the clucking of chickens and the fluttering of their feathers. The *attacca* marking at the end of this piece was omitted by Rimsky-Korsakov and many subsequent editions.

"Samuel" Goldenberg and "Schmuÿle" 39

Original title in Yiddish: *"Samuel" Goldenberg und "Schmujle"*
Stasov's comment: *Two Polish Jews, the one rich and the other poor.*

This is a consummate musical caricature in which Moussorgsky insultingly fuses two derogatory Jewish stereotypes into one representation. The first one is the rich, pompous, arrogant and assimilated Jew ("Samuel"), who "speaks" in an imperative and assertive fashion in the opening section. The theme is decisive and highly ornamented. The second ("Schmuÿle," Yiddish for Samuel) represents the *zhidy*, which is an offensive Russian epithet for Jews. These were the commonly encountered Diaspora Jews who clung to their Hebraic traditions and were stereotyped as poor, rootless, greedy and contemptible. They "speak," in the second section, in the chanting high voice used during ritual *davening* (praying) in the synagogue. Musically, this is communicated by a theme comprised of constant 16th-note triplets and eighth notes in the upper register of the piano. The first and second themes are fused together in the final section. This piece was undoubtedly inspired by two pencil drawings given by Hartmann to Moussorgsky, who in turn lent them to the gallery for the Memorial Exhibition. They were listed in the catalog as *"A rich Jew wearing a fur hat"* and *"A poor Sandomir Jew."* The fusion of these two stereotypical Jews is signified by placing quotation marks on both "Samuel" and the equivalent Yiddish name "Schmuÿle." It was as if to say, *"You can be a pretentious 'Samuel' by putting on fine clothes and attempting to be Europeanized, but at heart you are a poor, whining little 'Schmuÿle.'"*

A Rich Jew in a Fur Hat
Pencil, sepia and lacquer by Victor A. Hartmann

[30] Frankenstein, 283.

Moussorgsky had an interesting and ambivalent relationship with the Jewish people who appear in his music (not always in a good light) at a time in history which saw severe oppression and discrimination. Russian *pogroms*[31] began in earnest following the assassination of Alexander II in 1881. Although the assassin was not a Jew, the Jews were used as scapegoats to divert a discontented populace. Many scholars describe Moussorgsky as anti-Semitic, which would not be unusual among those of his aristocratic social background. Author and film historian Jay Leyda, in his book, wrote:

> All Moussorgsky letters that have been included are translated intact—with one qualification: at the risk of joining Moussorgsky's editorial "cleansers" we have omitted violently chauvinist phrases directed against Jews and Catholics as groups. Moussorgsky's anti-Semitism and anti-Catholicism derived from his unthinking adherence to the nationalist program laid down by Balakirev and Stasov.[32]

Poor Jew (An Old Man)
pencil, watercolor by Victor A. Hartmann

At the same time, his virulence with respect to the *zhidy* contrasted with his admiration for the *yevrei* (a Russian term for the heroic biblical Hebrews or Israelites).[33]

Moussorgsky composed moving testimonials to Jewish history, tradition, religion and character with many compositions based on Old Testament and Hebraic writings. In September 1879, he wrote to Stasov, "...in Odessa, I went to holy services at two synagogues, and was in raptures. I have clearly remembered two Israelite themes: one sung by the cantor, the other by the temple choir—the latter in unison; I shall never forget these!"[34]

Moussorgsky's original title *"Samuel" Goldenberg und "Schmuÿle"* was probably suppressed because of alleged derogatory references to Jews. Stasov used the non-derogatory title, *Two Jews, One Rich, the Other Poor*, in his obituary to Moussorgsky in 1881. Authors and editors such as Pavel Lamm, Emilia Fried, Alfred Frankenstein, Alfredo Casela, and Jay Leyda and Sergei Bertensson have utilized the "cleansed" title, which is consistent with broad Soviet era attempts to suppress anti-Semitic references in published creative works. However, the correct title, *"Samuel" Goldenberg und "Schmuÿle,"* is written in the autograph manuscript in Moussorgsky's own hand.

Limoges. The Marketplace (The Big News) 44

Original title in French: *Limoges. Le marché (La grande nouvelle)*
Stasov's comment: *Frenchwomen furiously disputing in the marketplace.*

Hartmann painted many watercolors in the town of Limoges, most of them of the famous cathedral. Nearly 75 were listed in the Exhibition Catalog; however, none were of the marketplace or the women in them. They were probably Moussorgsky's invention. This is a wonderful portrayal of French market women furiously gossiping, chattering and quarreling behind their carts. Two brief introductory texts written in French were found in the autograph under the title. They were crossed out by Moussorgsky:

> The Big News: Monsieur Pimpant from Panta-Pantaléon has found his cow—the one that ran away. "Yes, Madame, that was yesterday. —No, Madame, it was the day before yesterday. —Well, Madame, the cow was astray in the neighborhood. —No, Madame, the cow was not astray at all..."

> The Big News: Monsieur de Puissangeout has found his cow "Runaway." But the good women of Limoges will have nothing whatsoever to do with this incident because Mme. de Remboursac has acquired very fine porcelain dentures, while on the other hand Mr. De Panta-Pantaléon's obtrusive nose obstinately remains as red as a peony.

This piece is very rewarding for pianists to perform. While quite challenging, it is very pianistic.

[31] *Pogrom* (Russian: devastation or riot), a mob attack either approved or condoned by authorities, against the persons and property of a religious, racial or national minority. The term is usually applied to attacks on Jews in the Russian Empire in the late-19th and early-20th century (*The New Encyclopaedia Britannica, Micropaedia, Ready Reference*, vol. 9, 543).
[32] Leyda and Bertensson, xiv.
[33] Richard Taruskin, *Musorgsky: Eight Essays and an Epilogue* (Princeton, NJ: Princeton University Press, 1993), 380.

[34] Leyda and Bertensson, 394.

Paris Catacombs *(with the figures of V. A. Hartmann,
V. A. Kenel and a guide with a lantern)*
Watercolor by Victor A. Hartmann

Catacombs (A Roman Burial Chamber) 49

Original title in Latin: *Catacombae (Sepulcrum romanum)*
Stasov's comment: *Hartmann's picture shows the artist himself viewing
the Paris Catacombs by the light of a lantern.*

The Exhibition Catalog contained the following description
of this picture: *"Interior of Paris catacombs with figures of
Hartmann, the architect Kenel, and the guide holding a lamp."*[35]
There is a pile of skulls on the right. The watercolor is preserved and in the Russian museum in Leningrad. The
catacombs symbolize death and the helplessness of humans
to fight its inevitability. Death is a theme in much of
Moussorgsky's creative output, and toward it he had an
almost pathological fascination. The slow, sustained chords
that alternate between *ff* and *p* give the effect of an echo in
the cave. There is little or no melody and no key signature,
probably because of the vague tonality. The *attacca* at the end
is omitted in some editions and in Ravel's orchestration.

With the Dead in a Dead Language 50

Original title in Latin: *Con Mortuis in Lingua Mortua*

This title in Latin text precedes this piece; Moussorgsky wrote
it in pencil directly after the *attacca* of *Catacombs*. In the right-
hand margins he wrote the following note in Russian:

> *A Latin text: with the dead in a dead language. Well may
> it be in Latin! The creative spirit of the departed Hartmann
> leads me toward the skulls and addresses them—a pale light
> radiates from the interior of the skulls.*[36]

The lyrical theme is a variant of the *Promenade* theme and
serves as a sort of epilogue. Both *Catacombs* and *With the
Dead in a Dead Language* are introspective and show
Moussorgsky's reaction to Hartmann's death. In this piece,
pianists encounter the challenge of keeping the right-hand
tremolo sustained and even.

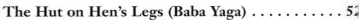

The Hut on Hen's Legs (Baba Yaga) . . . . 5?

Original title in Russian: *Izbushka na Kur'ikh Nozhkakh (Baba Yaga)*
Stasov's comment: *Hartmann's sketch depicted a clock in the shape of Baba
Yaga's hut on chicken's legs. Moussorgsky added the witch's ride in a mortar.*

Baba Yaga is the witch of Russian folklore. She rides through
the woods on a mortar (used to press wheat in olden times)
driven by a pestle and uses a broom to eliminate traces of her
path. Her hut is on chicken claws, which enable her to turn
in either direction to lure an approaching person into her
house. Once inside, she eats them and crushes their bones in
the mortar with her pestle. Hartmann's drawing is a design
for a Russian 14th-century clock made of bronze and colored
enamel and covered with an ornate design depicting animals
and fairy tales. It is preserved in the State Public Library in
Leningrad. This is one of the few virtuoso pieces in the
cycle. The driving rhythm of the octaves in the first and last

Baba Yaga's Hut on Hen's Legs (a clock in Russian style)
Pencil sketch by Victor A. Hartmann

sections gives the impression of the ticking of a clock. The
figurations are descriptive and confer an elemental power
upon the entire movement. The composer uses wonderful
colors, sonorities and dynamics to create the mysterious
atmosphere of the middle section.

---

[35] Richard Anthony Leonard, *A History of Russian Music* (London:
Macmillan Company, 1956), 112.
[36] Ibid., 112.

Design for Kiev City Gate (Main facade)
Pencil, watercolor by Victor A. Hartmann

The Bogatyr Gate (In the Ancient Capital, Kiev) . . . 61

Original title in Russian: *Bogatyrskie Vorota (vo stol nom gorode vo Kieve)*
Stasov's comment: *Hartmann's sketch represented his architectural project
for a city gate for Kiev in the old solid Russian style with a cupola in the
shape of a Slavic helmet.*

Hartmann entered a competition for a gate that was to be constructed to commemorate the escape of Czar Alexander II from an assassination attempt by a young revolutionary, Dmitry Karakozov, in the spring of April, 1866. The competition was called off and the gate was never built. Nevertheless, Hartmann considered his design to be his finest work. The name *Bogatyr* refers to mythological Russian heroes that lived in Kiev and made hunting their chief occupation. This last piece of the cycle incorporates ringing bells, a Russian chorale (*As You Are Baptized in Christ* appears in the two sections marked *senza espressione*), and the powerful return of the opening *Promenade* theme (measures 97–104), which binds the whole work together. The term *senza espressione* in measures 30 and 64 is a rare marking in keyboard notation—to this editor's knowledge, it is the first time this term appeared in a keyboard score. Ravel also made use of the term in *Le Gibet*, one of the three pieces in *Gaspard de la Nuit* written in 1908. Although he never met Moussorgsky, Ravel was influenced by the Russian School and was thoroughly familiar with *Pictures at an Exhibition* through his orchestration of the work. This musical picture is unsurpassed in grandeur and majesty and possesses unquestionable Russian national character.

Acknowledgments

I am deeply grateful to the following individuals for their encouragement and expert counsel in the preparation of this edition: Stewart Gordon, Professor and Chair of Keyboard Studies, Flora Thornton School of Music, University of Southern California, Los Angeles; Alan Smith and Kevin Fitz-Gerald, Professors of Keyboard Studies and Keyboard Collaborative Arts, Flora Thornton School of Music, University of Southern California, Los Angeles; James Bonn and Malcolm Hamilton, Professors Emeriti of Keyboard Studies, Flora Thornton School of Music, University of Southern California, Los Angeles; Constance Keene, Professor of Piano, Manhattan School of Music, New York; pianist Cécile Ousset, Paris, France; pianist Robert Macsparran for his tireless help in proofreading the musical engravings; my students, Juliane Song Lee and Jung Won Jin; Hughes Huffman, Administrative Coordinator, Flora Thornton School of Music, University of Southern California, Los Angeles; Alan Aaronson, Los Angeles; Ann Pope, Los Angeles; Kyril Glaidkovsky, Russia/Los Angeles, Marianne Visser, Amsterdam, The Netherlands for their translations of my research materials; and to Sherwyn M. Woods M.D., Ph.D., for his research of Russian Jewish history and tradition.

A very special thanks goes to Sharon Aaronson, Senior Masterwork Editor, Alfred Publishing, for her inspiration, enthusiasm, expertise and extraordinary dedication in the preparation of this edition.

I also wish to express my appreciation and gratitude to Charles Sens, Music Specialist, Music Division of the Library of Congress, Washington, DC for providing me with photocopies of the facsimile of *Pictures at an Exhibition*.

Nancy Bricard, La Quinta, California, 2002

Dedicated to Vladimir Vasilyevich Stasov
in memory of Victor Hartmann

PICTURES AT AN EXHIBITION
(1874)

PROMENADE

Modest Moussorgsky
(1839–1881)

ⓐ The sonority of these single notes is enhanced by pedaling.

ⓑ The *tenuto* under the A-flat is missing in most editions. It is found in the autograph.

ⓒ In Ravel's orchestral score, he adds a *mf*.

attacca

ⓓ This chord is incorrectly spelled with an F instead of a
D in some editions. The D is found in the autograph.

GNOME

(a) Original title in Latin: *Gnomus*

(b) Play the grace notes in this measure and in measures 30 and 35 almost simultaneously with the quarter notes to create an expressive dissonance.

ⓒ The autograph shows C-flats in both the upper and lower staves in this measure:

Rimsky-Korsakov changed the C-flats to B-flats. This editor has printed Rimsky-Korsakov's version on the premise that this measure should be consistent with measures 9 and 16.

ⓓ The autograph and the Rimsky-Korsakov editions show an octave G-flat in the upper staff. In the Moscow and many other editions, this octave was changed to F, probably to make the intervals analogous with the corresponding measure 53.

ⓔ The following measure was written after measures 44 and 53 and was deleted by Moussorgsky in the autograph:

(f) These E-flats (found in the autograph) do not correspond with the D-naturals in measure 45 or the parallel sequence in measure 54. In his orchestration of *Pictures at an Exhibition*, Ravel used the D-naturals:

(g) The following eight measures were written after measure 59 and were deleted by Moussorgsky in the autograph:

(h) The **Meno mosso** tempo head, which was written over the deleted measures in the autograph (see previous example), obviously applies to the music that followed.

(i) In the autograph, the octave grace notes in measure 66 were written before the bar line. This is misleading, as they begin the melody, which has just moved to the left hand.

ⓙ In this measure and measure 74, play the downbeat first with the left hand, then trill with the right hand. Continue the trill without accenting or stopping on the first 16th note in measures 73, 75, 77, 79, 81, 83 and 85.

ⓚ The notes in the lower staff in measures 73, 75, 77, 79, 81, 83 and 85 are written as 16th notes in all editions instead of 32nd notes, which are found in the autograph. This was obviously done because the use of 32nd notes left these measures one-half beat short. To correct this, an 8th note has been added in parentheses before the group of 32nd notes.

ⓛ In the autograph, Moussorgsky stopped the phrase line on the last 32nd note in measures 79, 81, 83 and 85. This edition extends those phrase lines to the trill in the next measure to be consistent with measures 74, 76 and 78. This achieves the overall intended sound effect.

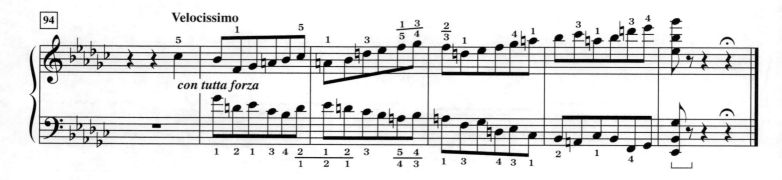

(m) Many editions erroneously place the *cresc.* at the beginning of the measure:

(n) In an attempt to fix the trill spelling to correctly lead into the next chord, Moussorgsky inadvertently creates a new problem as the B-double-flat needs to trill to some kind of C. Though not notated, C-double-flat is the best choice, which would give good reason for the C-flat reminder in the following measure:

PROMENADE

(a) This *p* is in the autograph but omitted in the Rimsky-Korsakov and many other editions.

ⓑ Most editions erroneously put a flat sign in front of the D, although there is no flat in the autograph.

Note the D-naturals in the similar chords on beat 4 in measure 10, right hand, and measure 12, left hand.

ⓒ The Rimsky-Korsakov edition and many other editions erroneously omit the natural sign in front of the D, even though it is found in the autograph.

ⓓ In the autograph, Moussorgsky has written an F instead of E-flat. Rimsky-Korsakov made the correction to E-flat, followed by all other editions except the Lamm edition.

THE OLD CASTLE

Andantino molto cantabile e con dolore ♪. = 56

(a) Original title in Italian: *Il vecchio Castello*

(b) Listen carefully to the length of all *portato* notes and be sure to hold them for their full value.

(c) Some editions incorrectly make this quarter note an 8th note, most likely because the preceding 8th rest in the autograph has a flourish on its tail, making it look like a backward quarter rest. It is a quarter note in the autograph.

(d) In the autograph, Moussorgsky adds an 8th rest after
the dotted-quarter note in the upper staff (but not in the
lower staff), which adds an extra beat to the measure:

The score has been corrected.

It is interesting to observe, however, that in measure 73, he notates quarter notes
instead of dotted-quarter notes in both staves.

(e) In the autograph, Moussorgsky begins this phrase on the upbeat D instead of on the downbeat of the following measure, as is found in measures 8, 19, 51 and 96. This may be due to the notation change in the upper voice of the bass clef, which extends an additional measure before the main theme returns.

(f) Some editions have changed this E to D-sharp to make it analogous to measure 53:

Moussorgsky has written an E in the autograph.

(g) Rimsky-Korsakov's edition and many editions that followed substitute a B-natural for the A-sharp that is found in the autograph, thus destroying the chromatic descent:

PROMENADE

(a) Play these 8th notes detached and without pedal. In his orchestration, Ravel marks them *pizzicato*.

TUILERIES (a)

(Dispute of Children after Play)

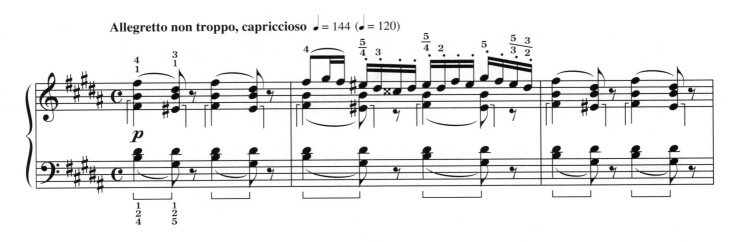

(a) Original title in French: *Tuileries (Dispute d'enfants après jeux)*

(b) Alternate *divisi* and fingering for measures 8 and 9:

(c) Some editions have a G-natural instead of G-sharp here and in measure 9, even though the autograph clearly shows a sharp in both measures. This error originated in the Rimsky-Korsakov edition.

(d) For those having difficulty rolling or playing the first chord of measure 13 in tempo, a solution is to tie the D-sharps between measures 12 and 13:

(e) One can envision a nana talking to the quarrelling children.

(f) The children respond with a laugh.

(g) Most editions have changed Moussorgsky's E-sharp to an F-sharp:

However, this editor feels that the E-sharp is preferable, not only for the harmonic voice leading, but also because it doesn't anticipate the F-sharp in the next measure.

(h) In measures 20–21 of the autograph, Moussorgsky mistakenly writes ♩. ♪♪♪ instead of ♩ ♪♪♪ The score has been corrected here.

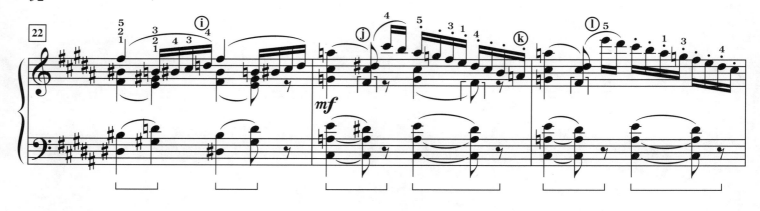

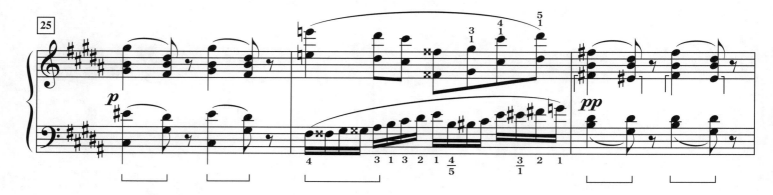

ⓘ In some editions the natural sign in front of the D is erroneously omitted. It is in the autograph.

ⓙ Moussorgsky's original phrasing in the right hand is shown in the score. Many editors have changed the original phrasing in measures 23 and 24 as follows:

or

ⓚ The natural sign is missing in the autograph in front of this right-hand A.

ⓛ This slur and the following right-hand *staccatos* have been added here to correspond with measure 23.

ⓜ Although this figure has been established without a tie in measures 2, 4, 12 and the beginning of measure 28, some editions tie the B's in this measure.

ⓝ Rimsky-Korsakov and other editions change this B-natural to an A-sharp:

The A-sharp is incorrect; the B-natural is written in the autograph.

CATTLE

ⓐ Original title in Polish: *Bydlo*

ⓑ Rimsky-Korsakov has replaced Moussorgsky's **ff** with a **p** followed by a 37-measure *poco a poco cresc.* Many subsequent editions, as well as the orchestration by Ravel, include this marking.

ⓒ Rimsky-Korsakov has replaced Moussorgsky's
8th-note chord and 8th rest with a quarter-note chord:

PROMENADE

(a) All editions except the Casella edition carry the *8va* to the end of measure 2, as found in the autograph:

The term *loco,* which Moussorgsky placed at the beginning of the next measure, supports that indication. Nevertheless, this editor believes that he did not intend to change registers at that point in the melody and has kept the melodic line consistent with measure 4.

BALLET OF THE UNHATCHED CHICKS [a]

[a] Original title in Russian: *Balet Nevylupivshikhsya Ptentsov*

D.C. il Scherzino, senza Trio, e poi Coda

ⓑ In the Rimsky-Korsakov and in many other editions, the upper auxiliary note for each trill in measures 23–30 is placed before the principal note:

For this reason, many pianists begin the trills on the upper auxiliary. This is incorrect, as Moussorgsky expressly notated these trills to begin on the principal note, with the upper auxiliary following.

"SAMUEL" GOLDENBERG AND "SCHMUŸLE" ⓐ

ⓐ Original title in Yiddish: *"Samuel" Goldenberg und "Schmujle"*

ⓑ In measures 1–9, Moussorgsky depicts a rich, pompous and arrogant Jew.

ⓒ In many editions this upbeat has been incorrectly made into a 32nd note instead of a 64th note (see example in footnote ⓓ).

ⓓ Rimsky-Korsakov began a tradition of errors by making triplets out of these three beamed 16th notes, causing the measure to be a 16th note short. Many subsequent editions include this error:

The Schirmer edition kept the incorrect triplet but changed the final two note values to a dotted-16th and 32nd note:

ⓔ Moussorgsky did not double-dot these 16th rests, necessary to compensate for the following 64th note. The additional dot has been added in the score.

ⓕ The Rimsky-Korsakov edition shows the note value for the upbeat to measure 7 as a 32nd rather than a 64th note, probably to compensate for Moussorgsky's error mentioned in the previous footnote.

(g) In measures 9–16, Moussorgsky depicts a poor, old and self-pitying Jew *davening* (reciting prayers) at the Wailing Wall.

(h) This double-flat found in the autograph is necessary only as a reminder. It is missing from many editions.

(i) Pedal indications here and in measure 12 are Moussorgsky's.

(j) This octave 16th is sometimes erroneously written as a 32nd note.

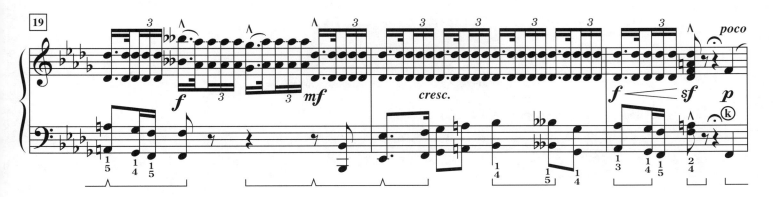

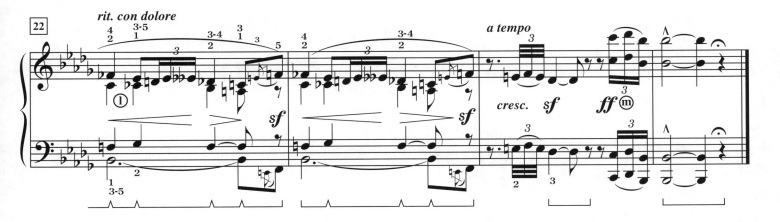

(k) Rimsky-Korsakov doubles the bass F in the tenor voice:

(l) Rimsky-Korsakov omits the flat sign in front of this C. This was probably an engraving error but many editions have perpetuated it. Also, on the last beat of measures 22 and 23, Moussorgsky did not reinstate the C-natural. The natural sign has been added in this score.

(m) Rimsky-Korsakov has changed the octave B-flats in this triplet to C, like the pattern of the preceding triplet that begins the measure.

PROMENADE

Ⓐ This **f** does not appear in the autograph but many editions add it. The character of this *Promenade* certainly calls for this dynamic marking so it has been added in parentheses.

ⓑ Rimsky-Korsakov substituted an octave G in the bass for the octave B-flat that is found in the autograph.

ⓒ All published editions carry this C major chord:

However, on careful scrutiny of the autograph, it is the editor's opinion that Moussorgsky actually wrote a B-flat instead of a C, which is consistent with measure 21 in the opening *Promenade*.

ⓓ Many editions erroneously print D instead of B-flat:

LIMOGES. THE MARKETPLACE ⓐ
(The Big News)

ⓐ Original title in French: *Limoges. Le marché (La grande nouvelle)*

ⓑ The *sf* indications in measures 5 and 30 are placed exactly as they appear in the autograph. Pavel Lamm has changed their positions to be analogous with each other. This is incorrect:

ⓒ The consecutive *f* dynamic markings that appear under the first notes of the upward right-hand slurs in measures 8, 12, 14, 19–24 and 33–35 were probably used by Moussorgsky for emphasis.

(d) In many editions this F-sharp is mistakenly omitted:

(e) Many editions have incorrectly printed a C instead of an E:

(f) This editor has added slurs to the last two 16th notes of measures 16, 17 and 21 as well as to the last six 16th notes in measure 24. These slurs are not found in the autograph.

(g) Alternate *divisi* and fingering: measure 17:   measure 18:   measure 19:

(h) This flat sign in front of this F is mistakenly omitted in many editions.

ⓘ For the first four 16th notes in the left hand in this measure and measure 34, Rimsky-Korsakov substituted an E-flat/G interval for Moussorgsky's D/F:

Presumably, Rimsky-Korsakov wished to make this measure analogous with measure 2, or perhaps he felt that starting this section on the dominant was weak. Many editions continue to print this change.

ⓙ This flat sign in front of the A has been added by the editor, although it is not in the autograph. Moussorgsky cancelled the right-hand A-flat at the beginning of the measure and probably forgot to reinstate it here.

(k) This E-flat note is left out of some editions. It is found in the autograph.

CATACOMBS ⓐ
(A Roman Burial Chamber)

ⓐ Original title in Latin: *Catacombae (Sepulcrum romanum)*

ⓑ In both the Lamm and the Schandert/Ashkenazy editions, the tied B's (measures 4–5) and the C-sharp (measure 8) in the upper staff have been incorrectly stemmed, contrary to what appears in the autograph. This is very misleading, as these up-stemmed notes are the moving line, which must be projected. The *sf*'s found in measures 4, 6 and 8 serve to emphasize these moving inner voices. In measures 25 and 29 the *sf*'s stress the top melodic note.

ⓒ Some editions do not have this tie. It is in the autograph.

ⓓ Do not change pedal here, as the tremolo in the next "picture" evolves out of the fading sound in this last measure.

WITH THE DEAD IN A DEAD LANGUAGE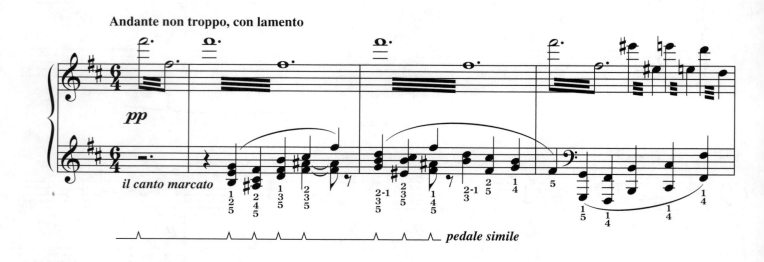

ⓐ Original title in Latin: *Con Mortuis in Lingua Mortua*

b Moussorgsky's original notation:

This edition clarifies Moussorgsky's cluttered notation by spreading to three staves and using whole notes rather than tied dotted-half notes.

Some editors who use Moussorgsky's original notation have unfortunately omitted the ties on the left-hand dotted-half notes:

c Many editions add *portato* markings in the left hand for this measure and measures 14 and 19:

THE HUT ON HEN'S LEGS  ⓐ
(Baba Yaga)

Allegro con brio, feroce ♩ = 120 (♩ = 144)

ⓐ Original title in Russian: *Izbushka na Kur'ikh Nozhkakh (Baba Yaga)*

ⓑ Many editions mark **sf** here instead of the **mf** found in the autograph.

ⓒ Many editions mark **cresc.** here instead of in measure 23, even though the autograph clearly shows two identical, four-measure patterns in measures 17–20 and 21–24.

ⓓ This **f** dynamic marking is missing in the autograph. It has been added here by analogy to measure 137. Many editions have **ff**.

(e) Rimsky-Korsakov has an A-sharp instead of Moussorgsky's F-sharp here. This is most likely an engraving error.

(f) The grace notes shown in this example, which were probably added by Rimsky-Korsakov, are found in measures 74 and 186 in many editions. They are written as *glissandi* in Ravel's orchestration.

(g) In some editions, the flat sign in front of the upper and lower E's at the beginning of measure 77 is absent:

This is probably an engraving error since E-flats are shown in analogous measures 78, 80, 81, 187, 189, 190, 192 and 193.

ⓗ Pedal indications in measures 108–109 and 112–113 are Moussorgsky's.

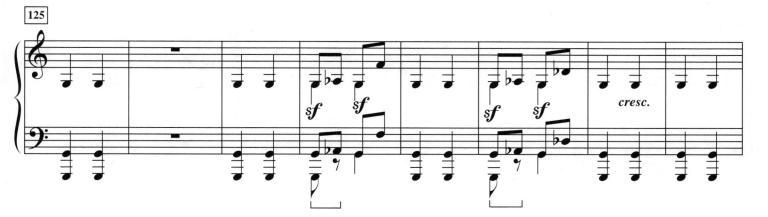

(i) The 13 measures in this example originally followed measure 122. Moussorgsky deleted them in ink and covered them over with a glued strip.

ⓙ Measures 21–24 are omitted in this return of the first section.

ⓚ Many editions have *ff* instead of Moussorgsky's *f*.

ⓛ Measures 29 and 30 are omitted in this return of the first section.

ⓜ Measures 141–142 are not found in the first section.

ⓝ A few editions have this wrong chord:

⊙ Because of the dramatic effect of the measures preceding the **attacca,** do not break the forward motion by changing the pedal until the beginning of *The Bogatyr Gate.*

THE BOGATYR GATE
(In the Ancient Capital, Kiev)

(a) Original title in Russian: *Bogatyrskie Vorota (vo stol nom gorode vo Kieve)*

(b) In measures 6 and 8, Rimsky-Korsakov has altered this B-flat root-position chord to a G minor first-inversion chord:

(c) The left-hand, inner-voice E-flat was omitted by Rimsky-Korsakov and other editions:
This could be an engraving error.

(d) At the end of measure 17, the autograph shows that Moussorgsky scratched out two measures that were a repeat of measures 16 and 17:

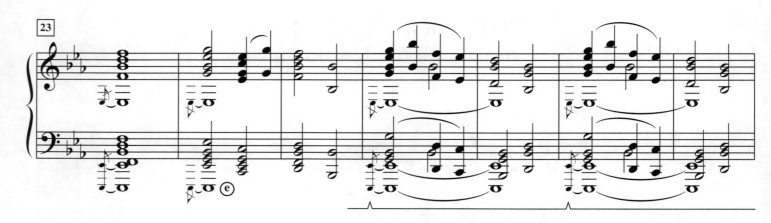

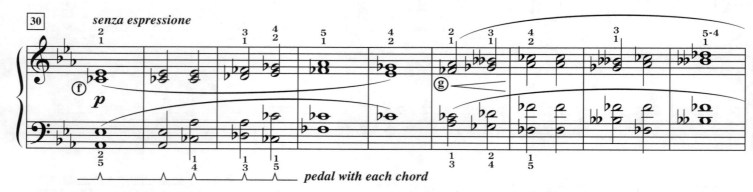

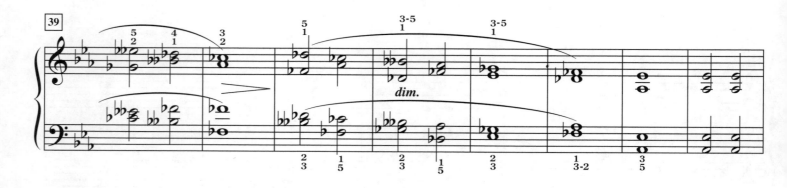

(e) Many editions tie the low E-flat whole notes in each staff to added whole notes in measure 25:

(f) Rimsky-Korsakov has added an A-flat in the soprano voice to this chord, presumably for a smoother melodic transition:

(g) The flat sign is missing in front of the F and a natural sign has been erroneously added in some editions:

The autograph shows an F-flat.

(h) This earlier version of measures 47–63 was found in the autograph underneath a glued strip containing the present version.

ⓘ An F instead of an E-flat is erroneously printed here in the Rimsky-Korsakov and other editions:

ⓙ Many editions have changed Moussorgsky's *ff* to a *p* to make the dynamics analogous with measure 30.

ⓚ Pedal indications in measures 81 and 82 are Moussorgsky's.

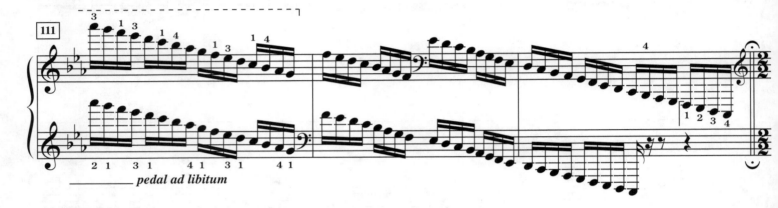

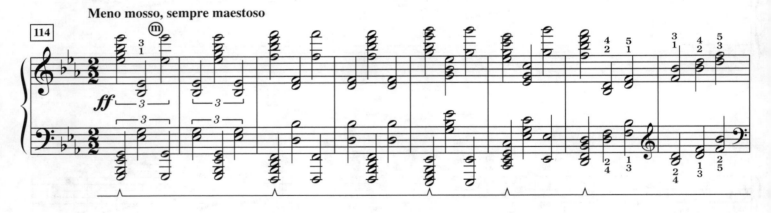

① Many editions erroneously print an F as the lowest note instead of Moussorgsky's E-flat:

This was probably an engraving error.

Ⓜ Rimsky-Korsakov and many other editions have filled in the right-hand chords on the last beat of measures 114, 116, 118 and 119:

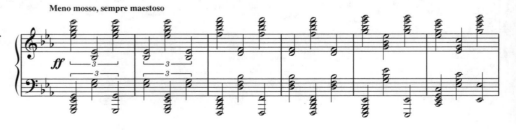

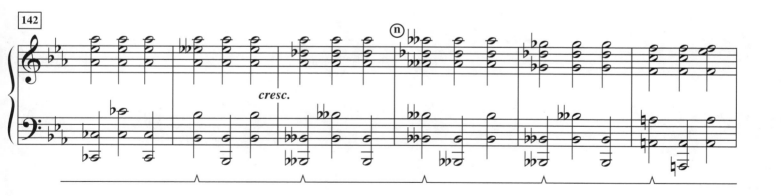

(n) In the upper staff in measure 145, instead of Moussorgsky's A-double-flat, Rimsky-Korsakov repeated the same chords found in the previous measure 144:

This alteration is found in many editions.

Ⓞ Rimsky-Korsakov added grace notes in measure 170, which are also found in many other editions.